Highlights **Puzzle Readers** | LEVEL **2**
LET'S READ, READ, READ

Kit and Kaboodle

GO CAMPING

By Michelle Portice
Art by Mitch Mortimer

HIGHLIGHTS PRESS
Honesdale, Pennsylvania

Stories + Puzzles = Reading Success!

Dear Parents,

Highlights Puzzle Readers are an innovative approach to learning to read that combines puzzles and stories to build motivated, confident readers.

Developed in collaboration with reading experts, the stories and puzzles are seamlessly integrated so that readers are encouraged to read the story, solve the puzzles, and then read the story again. This helps increase vocabulary and reading fluency and creates a satisfying reading experience for any kind of learner. In addition, solving Hidden Pictures puzzles fosters important reading and learning skills such as:

- shape and letter recognition
- letter-sound relationships
- visual discrimination
- logic
- flexible thinking
- sequencing

With high-interest stories, humorous characters, and trademark puzzles, Highlights Puzzle Readers offer a winning combination for inspiring young learners to love reading.

This is Kit.

This is Kaboodle.

They love to travel. You can help them on each adventure.

As you read the story, find the objects in each Hidden Pictures puzzle.

Then check the Packing List on pages 30-31 to make sure you found everything.

Happy reading!

Kit and Kaboodle want to go camping.

"Where should we go camping?"
asks Kaboodle.

"Let's look at the map," says Kit.
"This trail goes up to Mount Meow.
This trail goes down to Candy Canyon.
This trail goes along Rumble River."

"Let's hike up Mount Meow,"
says Kaboodle.

"Yippee!" says Kit. "I can't wait!"

"Let's pack," says Kaboodle.

Kit finds a small backpack.
"I hope this is not too big," she says.

Kaboodle finds a big backpack.
"I hope this is not too small," he says.

Kit packs a few things.
"I'm ready!" she says.

Kaboodle packs a few things.
Then he packs more things.

"There is so much to pack.
It will take hours!" he says.

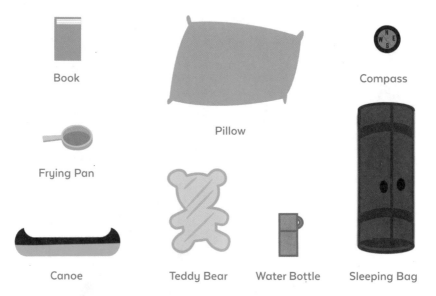

Book

Pillow

Compass

Frying Pan

Canoe

Teddy Bear

Water Bottle

Sleeping Bag

The next day, Kit and Kaboodle
go to the start of the trail.

"I hope I packed enough,"
says Kaboodle.

"I hope I did not pack too much,"
says Kit.

"Look up there," says Kit.

"The sun is shining on Mount Meow."

"I packed a few things we can use
to keep the sun out of our eyes,"
says Kaboodle.

He looks in his backpack.

Hat

Umbrella

Cowboy Hat

Bandana

Baseball Cap

Sunscreen

Visor

Sunglasses

Kit and Kaboodle hike into the forest.

"There is so much to see," says Kit.

"Let's play a game," says Kaboodle.

"I see a bug with six spots."

"I found it!" says Kit.

"I see a bug with five spots."

"I found it!" says Kaboodle.

"I'm getting tired," says Kaboodle.
"Let's take a break."

"Look over there," says Kit.
"I see a log where we can rest."

"I packed a few yummy snacks,"
says Kaboodle.

He looks in his backpack.

Graham Cracker

Marshmallow

Hot Dog

Celery

Apple

Grapes

Chocolate Bar

Cookie

"Wow," says Kit. "Look at the clouds."

"The clouds are so fluffy,"
says Kaboodle.

"I see a cloud that looks like a flower," says Kit.

"I see a cloud that looks like a sheep," says Kaboodle.

"Look up ahead," says Kaboodle.
"I see the campsite."

"Let's pitch the tent," says Kit.
"I see the perfect spot."

"I packed a few helpful tools,"
says Kaboodle.

He looks in his backpack.

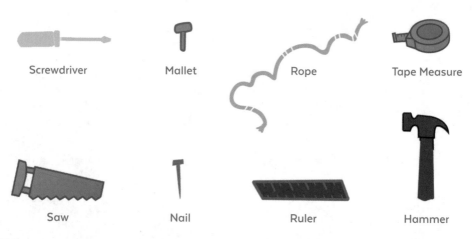

Screwdriver   Mallet   Rope   Tape Measure

Saw   Nail   Ruler   Hammer

Kit and Kaboodle work together
to pitch their tent.

They make a campfire.

"Let's roast marshmallows," says Kit.

"Here is a chocolate bar and a cracker,"
says Kaboodle.
"Let's put them all together."

"Yum!" says Kit.

"Look at the sky," says Kit.
"There are so many stars!"

"I packed a few things
we can use to see the stars,"
says Kaboodle.

He looks in his backpack.

Binoculars

Microscope

Telescope

Camera

Lantern

Magnifying Glass

Eyeglasses

Flashlight

"That group of stars looks like a little bear," says Kit.

"That group of stars looks
like a big bear," says Kaboodle.

"Camping is fun!" says Kit.

"What a nice trip," says Kaboodle.

"We make a good team," says Kit.

"Where should we go
on our next trip?" asks Kaboodle.

Hot-Air Balloon

Tractor

Sailboat

Airplane

Bicycle

Helicopter

Car

Train

Did you find all the things Kit an

Airplane

Apple

Bandana

Baseball Cap

Canoe

Car

Celery

Chocolate Bar

Flashlight

Frying Pan

Graham Cracker

Grapes

Hot-Air Balloon

Lantern

Magnifying Glass

Mallet

Rope

Ruler

Sailboat

Saw

Tape Measure

Teddy Bear

Telescope

Tractor